The Fairy
of the
Pink Lotus

inspired by Chinese folklore

The Fairy
of the
Pink Lotus

inspired by Chinese folklore

Katina Ivanova

Títle: The Fairy of the Pink Lotus
Subtitle: inspired by Chinese folklore
Copyright © Katina Ivanova 2021
Artwork by: artsroom1111@gmail.com
Artwork website: ksartists.wordpress.com
Copyright © Erik Istrup Publishing 2021
Published through IngramSpark.com
Font: MyriadPro
ISBN: 978-87-92980-72-4

Age: 4 - 9

This book will bring support for children who live in poor condition

Erik Istrup Publishing
Jyllandsgade 16 st. th., 9610 Nørager, Danmark
www.erikistrup.dk/publishing/ • eip@erikistrup.dk

5

On the next page
you can add your name
or a friends name on the banner

Part 1

Ancient Chinese heritage and folk tales inspired the story

In a secret place lived the fairy of the pink lotus. There, every morning, the first rays of the sun reflected with their shimmering pearly drops. Hundreds of small fish lived in the lake, dragonflies with glowing wings and small water ants that swam on the surface of the water with their small feet.

Thousands of pink lotus flowers have covered the waters of the beautiful lake since time immemorial. These lotuses regularly whispered to each other when the light breeze swayed them. The fairy of the pink lotus loved to listen to their sounds and their gossiping, the little rustling that turned into a real gentle rhapsody when the wind from the South intensified.

The fairy was tiny, but she managed to circle around between the thousands of flowers across the lake. She stepped on their pink bellies and laughed with joy. Even if she staggered, she would fall on her belly inside the flower which made her thrilled.

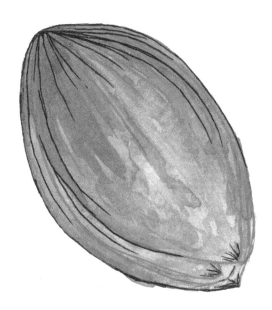

There were paths of small white and brown pebbles along the shore of the lake. That path stretched all the way to the nearby evergreen forest.

As the sun lit up the fairy of the pink lotus, a small dimple appeared on one of her cheeks, right next to her sweet pink smiling lips. The blue sky caressed the White Mountain in the distance, and the little clouds touched its tops. There gathered the little birds that fluttered the clouds with the tips of their small wings. The fairy loved to calm down and snuggle in the blossom of a flower in the lake as she looked up at the little birds, which kept singing and chasing each other in the air. She really liked their nonsense.

Around noon, the thirsty forest dwellers arrived at the lake. They were all friends with the pink lotus fairy, and after drinking water, they sat by the flowers to enjoy the beautiful view.

The fairy's favourite white rabbit could make original faces and stand on its hind legs, could move its long white moustache in rhythm, and could sneeze authoritatively, even when it didn't need to sneeze.

A mother mouse took all of her eight children to see the beautiful fairy. After the visit, they decided to each take a white stone away with them. Every day eight new pebbles were piled up together until they built their new home.

The fairy loved to bathe in the warm crystal clear water. Her dress was just as a pink lotus flower. When she fell asleep at night, she wrapped the robe around herself so she could hide. Hidden like this, it looked like a closed lotus flower, and when one looks at the closed lotus flowers in the lake in the evening, one could never recognize her.

Saturday was a very special day for the pink lotus fairy. She chose a nice sunny place and organizes herself a picnic. She ate sweet sandwiches with honey, made her own combination of walnuts and various other nuts and seeds that were so crunchy and delicious, drank fresh water with a mint leaf. The fairy loved big red juicy apples and ate them in large quantities. The fragrant lotuses toned her like that when she smells them! Saturdays were such happy days.

Suddenly a family of ducks appeared out of the blue. They had very beautiful colourful feathers and large shining eyes. It turned out that they had recently lost their home. A terrible man who poured a lot of gasoline into it with his boat polluted their swamp. It was no longer possible to live there. The lake with the pink lotuses is their new paradise. They will live in harmony with all its inhabitants.

The lotus fairy had a very gentle voice. She loved to sing songs. Her favourite song was the one about her beloved flowers - the pink lotuses. She loved them infinitely. Her gentle voice floated in the wind.

"My lotus, oh, my sweet lotus
Pink as the morning sky,
Be by my side now and
Be with me, forevermore!"

The little hummingbirds love to drink lotus flower nectar. Most of all, they like to rub the shiny drops of water on the lotus leaves. This water is so pure and refreshing that the little eyes of hummingbirds sparkle with happiness when they touch their beaks in the silver drops. They flutter fast and the sun burns hard, which is why they get thirsty so quickly. One drop is enough for a fresh, life-giving sip of the little bird. Along with them, the entire lake of water lilies celebrates the wonderful warm season.

Hummingbirds are magical birds. They speak and understand all foreign languages because they can fly far away around the world.

At night, darkness descends over the lake. Countless stars twinkle in the sky. Nobody knows their number. Crickets sing as the most faithful guardians of the night. Sometimes the pink lotus fairy doesn't want to sleep at all. She stands and listens to the wonderful music of the crickets and prays they never end their song because it is so pleasant.

One day in the early morning, someone played a bamboo flute nearby. The sound was so gentle and kind. The good tune came from a little boy playing. He was so good at it that all the inhabitants of the lake enjoyed it. The lotus fairy really liked the boy's song. After a few hours, the boy left. The fairy of the pink lotus was very sad. She wanted him to come back and play again. She wanted so badly to hear it again!

The next day the boy came again. He sat by the lake and played his beautiful song. He was a very nice boy. He had a white shirt and light blue pants. He was carrying a small bag on his back for the flute.

The fairy of the pink lotus listened to the boy's music and started dreaming. Suddenly the boy noticed her. She was most gentle, beautiful, and dreamy with closed eyes. He worried and stopped playing. The fairy opened her eyes. He introduced himself. She told him he was really a very talented musician. She asked him to play more. He whistled happily on his flute, smiling slightly.

So day after day the little boy came to play by the lake with the pink lotuses. His music revived everything in the lake, and the lotuses grew much faster. The entire lake was in fresh pink. The pink lotus fairy and the boy were very happy together. They had time to listen to beautiful music while watching the clear water with fresh pink flowers, talk and share different stories and dreams.

The lotus fairy waited impatiently for the boy with the flute every day.

One day the fairy was laughing at a funny story. The boy stared her straight. He seemed willing to share something with her, but he didn't know how. The lotus fairy looked

20

at him seriously. She asked him what was bothering him. The boy replied that for him she was the most beautiful creature in the world. He looked up at the sky and took a deep breath. He told her: "… your beauty… It fills my heart completely. And my lips are burning because I want to give you a million words of love." The lotus fairy worried and asked him to leave. He left.

The boy did not show up the next day. The fairy really wanted to see him, but she didn't know what to do.

After a few days, the boy returned to the lake. The fairy went to him and greeted him. He played his flute and his song was so beautiful. No one in the lake had heard a softer song. The lotus fairy turned to the boy and wasn't sure if he would love her so much forever. The fairy said it worried her because people love and then stop loving. She said there might be thousands of other girls who were more suitable for him. He insisted she was the only one for him and that he would never give up on her. They talked for a long time; they talked all night; he didn't want to give up the lotus fairy. Finally, the boy left. The lotus fairy had asked him if he would recognize her among the thousands.

The next day the boy came again. It poured. The rain turned into a big storm. The boy took her into a hollow of an old tree in the nearby forest. So they stayed dry inside it all night. Early before sunrise, the lotus fairy left the hollow and hid at home among the pink lotuses in the lake. In her rolled-up dress, she hid among the lotuses and was invisible.

In the morning, the boy woke up and ran to the lake to look for the fairy. He couldn't find her, but saw only the enormous lake with the thousands of lotus flowers. The boy did not know what to do. He stood alone and helpless on the shore of the lake. He was watching the lotuses. The boy watched for any movement. Nothing.

Suddenly the boy saw among the lotuses, which were covered with the drops of last night's rain, a lotus that was completely dry. That was SHE. He touched gently the fairy, and she appeared. Then he smiled and said, "Did you see I recognized you?"

The fairy also smiled and was glad that he recognized her among the thousands. From that day on, the fairy of the pink lotus and the boy with the bamboo flute never parted.

Part 2

Life in the lake of pink lotuses was very joyful. There was friendship, joy and love that you cannot find anywhere else. Everyone understands each other, and the entire lake around existed in complete harmony. The morning sun was touching gently the dimple of the fairy's smiling face. There were a lot of beautiful things to marvel at and smile to here. Her heart was calm and pure. She loved to laugh with the butterflies and to watch in curiosity their play from flower to flower.

The greatest deeds in the world begin with an initial moment.

That was the moment when the Blue Dragon arrived from the near White Mountains. The Blue dragon was huge, and the fairy was so tiny compared to him. The boy and the fairy had heard stories about dragons, but they had never met one live. A legend passed down from father to son, which the boy had heard from his father once, said:

"Of all the snakelike monsters, there is nothing scarier than the dragon.

He exhales terrible fiery flames. He has sharp teeth and clutches that can grab you. Also has a special spike at the end of his long tail with which he can hit or pierce anyone from a great distance.

Dragons are agile.

Besides flying dragons, there are water dragons.

They are very dangerous as well. They live in deep sea waters and cannot breathe fire. Their strength is to hide on the seabed and wait for their prey.

The legend told by the boy's father ends:

In fact, there was once a magic whistle that could calm and put to sleep any dragon. The whistle was strictly guarded by treasure hunters, and so no one has ever seen it. "

The little boy and the lotus fairy approached the Blue Dragon and introduced themselves. The dragon's gigantic eyes highly opened in surprise. His eyes were fearful and piercing. All the other inhabitants of the lake hid and fell silent in anticipation. The pink lotus fairy asked the dragon what brought him here.

The dragon told them he had lived in the nearby mountains for many years. He had recently lost his child and was now suffering, grieving and wandering around looking for him.

The baby dragon had hatched from its egg recently and was eager to explore the world. He's probably wandering somewhere of curiosity and can't find his way back home.

As he told his story, the Blue Dragon looked so sad, with eyes filled with huge tears. The dragon complained he felt all alone on earth and that he could not live without his baby.

The little boy got very touched about this story. He picked up his bamboo flute and played. It was a very pure, wonderful melody of love and compassion for the mother and her beloved child.

The boy's music opened Blue Dragon's heart. There was so much love and beauty in those sounds. The lake of thousands of pink lotuses seemed to reflect the music of the bamboo flute like a mirror to the bright blue sky. The dragon laid and closed his eyes. It seemed that the dragon, exhausted, lonely, and hopeless, has finally calmed down.

The boy continued to play with his lips, barely touching the flute. The melody seemed to appear on its own, enveloping everything around it in graceful tones that reached as far as the nearby forest. No one moved, and everyone listened in amazement to the magical music. The beautiful sounds fascinated the dragon the most, because it was the first time the dragon hearing the boy's music with the flute. This helped him to recover and gave so much hope and faith.

In a moment, the dragon slowly stood up. The Blue dragon drank a lot of the clear water from the lake to gather strength and energy. The Blue dragon turned to the boy and the fairy of the pink lotus and asked:

"Will you come with me to help me find my son?"

They both agreed and settled comfortably on the beast's large back. The dragon flew quickly to the nearby mountains. From so high, the lake with the thousands of lotuses looked so small. The entire lake looked like a single water lotus flower made by many flowers.

How the dragon's child could be lost? Where could it have gone?

As they approached the White Mountain, the air became chilly and wet. The pink lotus fairy shivered. But when she looked down, she couldn't help but admire this amazing view! Everything was wrapped in a soft white veil of snow. The trees were dressed in sparkling white wedding dresses, and small drops of ice and snowflakes gleamed on the surface of the earth.

The pink lotus fairy and the boy looked at each other -"Let's find him!"

The dragon flew very low, searching the area. They were flying slowly and carefully among the countless trees in silence. The boy took out his flute, starting to play it. The echo of his music stood out on the icy ground like a thousand copper bells.

It was so quiet that the music echoed far and wide. The music caught the squirrels' attention. In a short time, a large crowd of listeners gathered. The dragon slowly landed. Everyone gasped in surprise when they saw the little fairy and the boy on the back of the dragon.

With the help of the animals that gathered, it became clear that the baby dragon is alright and not lost. It is nearby with the eagle. The eagle is also trying to help him by flying high and looking for dragon's parents.

What a nice surprise! The blue dragon immediately flew and happily spread wings, rushed to his child. The blue dragon and the baby dragon were in a seventh heaven of happiness. Together again! They knew they would never separate from each other ever again!

The pink lotus fairy and the boy returned home. They had a lot to tell. They sat by the lake with their friends and told them all the story of the dragon baby's rescue mission. As they talked, they were eating salad, sweet biscuits and bright red juicy strawberries. The food is much tastier after a job well done. After they finished the story, the duck family said they were so proud of having such noble friends.

Part 3

There was complete harmony in the lake of the pink lotuses. The fairy was having fun in her favourite beautiful pose. She lay in the open lotus flower, staring at the bright blue sky. Suddenly a swarm of bees circled the sky. These small and beautiful creatures flutter their wings so fast. They shine in the sun like their wings are little golden feathers or pearls. The bees surrounded the pink lotus fairy. They started chatting with her.

The work of the bees is extremely important. They explained how many aromas and flavours there were in each flower they touched.

The flowers of the apple tree have beautiful pink stamens that can be smelled from afar. Their aroma is sweet. It brings a fresh and warm scent. From their scent, the bees can imagine tasting the sweet juicy apples. The fairy smiled and looked playfully. She loved juicy apples so much!

The bees kept educating. The lemon flowers are very tasty. When you smell them, they have life-giving energy and carry such a rich aroma. This aroma is absorbed by the leaves of the lemon tree as well. When the bees gather around the lemon tree, it sings with joy. The leaves and flowers vibrate from their joyful meeting with the bees. It is so cooling and pleasant among the leaves of fragrant lemons.

The bees love spring flowers. One of them is the daffodil. They adore it. The bees enthusiastically told the fairy how diverse and different the colours of the daffodil were. They can be white and yellow and also mixed and smell like spring. And this is one of the most pleasant sensations in the world.

Listening to the stories of the bees, the boy got excited and inspired. He picked up his bamboo flute and played his beautiful tune. As the boy played his flute, the bees continued to talk about their delicious and fragrant universe.

There is a great friendship between bees, and Chinese rose bushes. They have a magical bright red or pink colour and are so beautiful. In the colours of roses, the bees sometimes find many new and unfamiliar sensations. Feelings that the bees have never had before and that's why they learn about them by touching the rose flower. At such a moment, time seems to stop. As if you can feel the past. These flowers of the rose are so magical.

Sometimes, when one touches the rose flower, one can also feel this magic. It is as if time stops and the past is happening right now. It seems like stroking the wall of an ancient cave - mysterious, calm and eternal. Such were the sensations of touching the magical rose of eternity.

The boy with the bamboo flute felt that feeling. The melody of the flute reflected like the echo of a deep ancient cave. There were nuances of the cool grey and damp rocks inside the cave and the blue sunny sky that appeared through the cave's small openings. The boy's music became an entire story.

Then the bees continued on. There were small daisies sprouting among the thick green grass in the bees' stories. There were also tiny blackberry flowers that grow in the beautiful forest meadow, herbs, berries and much more. This was a whole wonderful cosmos of flavours and aromas.

The boy with the flute smiled and bowed. What wonderful friends the bees are! Ah, how much we can learn from them and from their care for plant life. That is why there is nothing tastier than golden forest honey! Especially if eaten in the company of friends.

The fairy completely agreed with the boy's opinion. She explained her experience with flowers. In this way, she wanted to share her charm of her favourite flower, the pink lotus. She needed to thank also the bees for their beautiful stories. The fairy said that when she touched the heart of the lotus flower; the drops moved and shone like little twinkling stars. This makes the fairy's heart flutter with happiness. The bees agreed this so amazing.

Part 4

Life in the lake of pink lotuses suddenly became restless. The lotus fairy's birthday was approaching. The animals were preparing hard to give her a surprise party. Mother mouse with her eight children competed to wear various flowers and make wreaths. They wanted to decorate the place of the event very festively and colourfully. They arranged colour wreaths on the ground. It looked like a flower carpet with many shapes and scents.

Then on this magical fragrant carpet the animals arranged all types of delicacies. There was wild mushroom soup, carrot cake, cherries, honey cakes, pumpkin pie with walnuts and lemonade for everyone.

The boy with the bamboo flute disappeared before sunrise that day. The animals thought he was cooking something for the birthday too. A little snail smiled secretly because he knew where the boy was. He had gone to town to get a present for the lotus fairy. When he returned, the boy was silent and said nothing to anyone. It looked very mysterious.

Here the celebration began. The fairy was so pleased with everything they had prepared for her. There was great gratitude in her eyes. The most important thing for her was she being with everyone she loved so much.

They almost finished the gala lunch when the boy stood up. He pulled out a tiny box of fine white porcelain from his bag. There were painted beautiful blue flowers and a tiny golden button to open it. The animals were very happy. Their eyes watered at the sight of this beautiful box. The box was made by a skilled craftsman of Chinese porcelain. He learned the trade from his father and grandfather, and they from their grandfathers.

The fairy's cheeks flushed with excitement. They looked like two ripe strawberries at the sight of this surprise. The boy looked at her in the eyes and whispered:

"I love you with all my heart. Happy birthday, dear! Here you are!"

The pink lotus fairy opened the box and gasped in surprise. There was a real pearl inside–as blue as the sky. The pearl was so beautiful and big! There were hundreds of flashes of the magical blue glowing sky into this pearl.

The End

CPSIA information can be obtained
at www.ICGtesting.com
Printed in the USA
LVHW072014071221
705520LV00007B/512